This

Book Belongs to

Órla

Read all about your favourite bear!

Once Upon a Time with Winnie the Pooh
Nursery Rhymes of Winnie the Pooh
My Very First Winnie the Pooh Treasury

Disney's
Celebrate the Year with
Winnie the Pooh

Ladybird

A Catalogue record for this book is available from the British Library.

Published by Ladybird Books Ltd.
27 Wrights Lane
LONDON
W8 5TZ

A Penguin Company

2 4 6 8 10 9 7 5 3 1

Ladybird and the device of a ladybird are trademarks of Ladybird Books Ltd.

Printed in Spain

http://www.ladybird.co.uk

Contents

Celebrate the Year
with Winnie the Pooh

Celebrating special days is the handing down of tradition. We learn all about Valentine's Day, Easter, April Fools' Day, Halloween, Thanksgiving, and Christmas through the shared experiences of family and friends. Celebrations offer opportunities to get together and have fun! It is therefore no wonder that Pooh and his friends lend themselves so easily to this book of special days. To delight in Pooh's world is to be constantly drawn to the caring that these characters possess for one another. Each one is concerned on some level about the gloominess of Eeyore, the well-being of Piglet, and the general confusion of the bear of little brain. Pooh and his friends are filled with questions, just like children. Here we present a selection of stories to share with children as Pooh and his friends discover the true meaning of some special celebrations.

Valentine's Day

Everybody loves to be loved! While love is shown in little things we do every day, on Valentine's Day it takes centre stage. What is most wonderful about Valentine's Day is how accessible it is to children and adults alike. An expression of love can be as simple as a heart drawn on a piece of paper, or it can be ornate, glowing radiantly or shimmering with rainbows. The love with which it is offered is more important than the way it looks.

By its very nature, a valentine is something special. Part of the message of Valentine's Day is inclusion and friendship. Children want to give valentines to everyone in their class; to everyone in the world!

In addition to making cards, it's fun to make valentine boxes that your children can use to hold the valentines they've received. These can be plain shoe boxes that are painted bright colours and decorated with hearts, doilies, tissue paper, and cut-out pictures of things they love. Everyone's valentine is different, and that's part of what makes it fun! In this story, when little Roo decides to give his mother a valentine, Pooh and his friends share Roo's discovery that there are many different ways to say, "I love you."

Valentine Boxes

You will need:
- a shoe box
- glue
- coloured tissue paper
- paper doilies
- magazine pictures
- scissors

Cut out pictures from magazines and make a collage on the sides of the box. Add doilies and tissue paper shapes, such as hearts, for a pretty layered effect. It's always nice to write the date somewhere on the box, too.

DISNEY's

Winnie the Pooh's Valentine

Bruce Talkington

Illustrated by John Kurtz

It was easy to see what day it was in the Hundred-Acre Wood. Birds cuddled in pairs and were loudly chirping duets. Friendly breezes tickled leaves on the trees until they fluttered with laughter. Saplings shyly touched and, bending close, exchanged sweet secrets in restless whispers. It always seemed, on Valentine's Day, that things were more tightly wrapped around each other than usual.

At Winnie the Pooh's house, things were taking on a decidedly "heartfelt" appearance, mostly because Pooh had just finished sticking hearts made from pink felt in all the most strategic places. Strategic, Owl had once explained, meant the places where things were sure to be in the way and, therefore, attract the most attention.

Pooh's happy contemplation of his handiwork was suddenly interrupted by a quiet voice saying "Pooh Bear" in a most polite tone.

Startled, Pooh turned so quickly that he bumped his nose on a soft felt heart tacked to the back of a very hard door.

"Oh, bother!" sniffed Pooh, as he noticed Roo standing anxiously in the middle of his sitting room. "Why, hello, little Roo!" he exclaimed.

"Hello, Pooh," replied Roo. "Is that felt?" he asked, pointing to the heart.

Pooh cautiously rubbed his nose. "Oh, I felt it, alright," he assured Roo woefully.

"No," said Roo, "is that heart felt?"

"Oh!" said Pooh, not really understanding the question. "No, I don't think the heart felt it at all."

Roo smiled brightly at the bear of very little brain and knew that it was time to talk about something else. "Would you mind terribly," he asked politely, "if we talk about something besides your felt hearts?"

"That would be wonderful," breathed Pooh in relief. "What did you have in mind?"

"I want to give a valentine to my mum," Roo whispered, "but I don't know how."

"Neither do I!" laughed Pooh, who was always delighted to agree with someone about something. But his laughter ceased as soon as he saw the look on little Roo's face.

"Then what'll I do?" piped Roo, feeling a distress so profound he could hardly keep his eyes from filling with tears.

"What *we* will do," said Pooh, taking Roo's tiny hand in his own, "is find out how!"

In no time at all, Pooh and Roo had gathered together all their best friends — Piglet, Tigger, Rabbit, Gopher, and, of course, Eeyore — and put Roo's question to them.

"Well," suggested Piglet in a very small voice, "the most important thing about a valentine is that it says 'I love you.'"

"Yes!" agreed Tigger, bouncing around the room in excitement. "And it's got to say it in bright colours!"

"Impressive!" added Gopher. "It's got to be impressive because saying 'I love you' is a pretty impressive thing."

"And because 'I love you' are the most important words one person can say to another," sniffed Rabbit knowingly, "a valentine should say them in as many different ways as possible."

"What do you think, Eeyore?" Pooh asked the donkey, who was being even more silent than usual.

"Well, since you're asking," mumbled Eeyore in his very slow way, "I suppose the sort of valentine you're planning is definitely one way of going about it."

"Then what are we waiting for?" hooted Tigger. "Christmas?"

"I'll get my tools," said Gopher gleefully.

"I'll get my dictionary," said Rabbit.

"I'll clean up afterwards," said Piglet.

"And I'll tell you what I think of it when it's finished," announced Eeyore, "if anyone is interested, that is."

Gopher chiselled a huge heart out of a boulder he had been saving for just such a special occasion. It was twice as tall as Tigger, even if he balanced on the very tip-top of his tail.

"Impressive," everyone told Gopher when, at last, he'd finished.

The irrepressible Tigger wasted not a moment painting the heart with the most spectacular colours he could think of, bright orange with black stripedy stripes.

"Posilutely splendiferous," Tigger purred when he'd completed his task.

And as Piglet swept up the work area, Roo climbed up onto the obliging Eeyore's back and wrote "I love you" on the heart in his very best writing. Everyone agreed that although it was very small as writing goes, it couldn't have been more neatly done.

Then, after consulting a dictionary so thick he'd had to carry it all the way from his house in a wheelbarrow, Rabbit added a great many words and phrases, including "Kiss me goodnight" and "Do your homework" and "Eat your vegetables," as well as "Smoochface," "Pookums," and — Rabbit's personal favourite — "Snugglebunny."

The completed valentine was an impressive, no, a magnificent, sight. The friends were all very pleased with themselves until Roo, after thinking for some time, suddenly blurted out, "But how am I going to get this to my mother?"

Spirits plummeted. No one had thought of how this valentine was going to be delivered to Kanga. Posting it was out of the question. Even if an envelope of the proper size could have been produced in time, the correct number of postage stamps would have weighed more than the valentine itself.

Sitting in a sad little circle, the friends were unable to come up with any useful ideas at all.

"I guess we'll just have to give up," sighed Tigger hopelessly.

"Then now's the time I'll tell you what I thought," announced Eeyore, "if you really want to know, that is."

"Oh, I think we really do want to know, Eeyore," said Pooh.

"I think," said Eeyore, "what I thought all along. This valentine is definitely *one* way of doing it."

"Why, Eeyore!" exclaimed Pooh. "I believe that's very helpful!"

"It is?" brayed the startled donkey.

"Certainly," explained Pooh, furrowing his brow. "If this is one way of doing a valentine, that means there must be a two way!"

Everyone exchanged amazed smiles and nods as Roo leaped excitedly to his feet.

"You're right, Pooh! You're right!" he shouted. "And I know exactly what the two way is, thanks to all of you!"

That evening at just about suppertime (according to the rumblings of Pooh's tummy), they all watched as Roo presented his mother, Kanga, with a handful of beautiful wild flowers. "These flowers," Roo explained to Kanga, "say 'I love you' . . ."

Pooh poked Piglet to make sure he'd heard, but the smile on Piglet's face told him that he hadn't missed a thing.

" . . . and," Roo continued, "they say it in very bright colours."

Tigger puffed out his chest so far he nearly fell off his tail.

"And because the flowers are all different kinds, they say 'I love you' in lots of different ways."

Rabbit remarked that he had something in his eye so no one should think he was crying or anything.

"And," said Roo, completing the presentation, "they're the most impressive valentine I could carry all by myself."

Gopher blew his nose into a brightly patterned handkerchief.

"Thank you, Roo, dear," smiled Kanga. Sniffing the flowers, she added, "I couldn't have asked for a more perfect valentine."

As mother and son embraced, Tigger leaned over to Pooh and whispered, "But what'll we do with the valentine we made?"

"Leave it exactly where it is," Pooh whispered back. "It will remind us that there can be a lot of love in every single day if you just know where to look for it!"

Easter

The celebration of Easter is the glory of renewal. Children themselves are the symbol of this reawakening. In this story, Pooh and his friends find a large egg and ponder its origin. Rabbit has heard that it is, in fact, an Easter egg that will eventually talk to them and tell everyone how much it cares for them. They wait and wait, but the egg doesn't speak. Pooh decides they should all paint themselves as Easter eggs in order to converse more easily with the egg when it does speak. Christopher Robin soon comes forward and shows how this particular Easter egg is a gift from him to all his friends.

Painting eggs and making paper baskets with children are just some of the ways we can celebrate Easter. If you have a garden or sunny windowsill, planting flowers in paper cups is also fun – although you have to wait for a little while before seeing the colourful results!

Easter Flowers

You will need:

★ plastic cups (clear, if possible, so you can see things grow) ★ multipurpose compost
★ seeds or small flowering plants such as petunias or pansies   ★ water

Fill the cups about 3/4-full with compost, making sure you don't pack it down too tightly. With your finger, make a little hole in the soil and drop in the seed or the roots of your plant. Gently fill up with soil, pour in a little water, and place on a sunny outside windowsill. When the seedlings break the surface or when the flowering plants start growing over the edge of the cup, it is time to transplant them to a larger pot.

DISNEY's

Winnie the Pooh's
Easter

Bruce Talkington

Illustrated by Bill Langley and Diana Wakeman

innie the Pooh felt a stirring to see the Hundred-Acre Wood in all its new spring finery. The magic of the season was shaking off the sleep of winter, so Pooh was climbing the path that led to a very special place called "Up There."

In the middle of the clearing Up There, perched on its large end, sat the biggest egg Pooh had ever seen!

My, thought Pooh, that egg is as tall as Christopher Robin. Perhaps taller!

Its size, however, wasn't the most surprising thing about the egg. It was all violet stripes and bright green squiggles, yellow polka dots, and pink swirls!

Pooh laughed out loud. Pooh's very good friends heard him laugh, and came to find out just what was so funny.

"Oh, my goodness," squeaked an amazed Piglet. "That is the most un-very-small egg I have ever seen!"

Gopher squinted and surveyed the egg carefully. "That's some breakfast!"

"This is nothing," chuckled Tigger. "But I bet the look on the chicken's face was something when she laid it! Hoo-hoo-hoo!"

"Oh, don't be silly," snapped Rabbit. "It's obvious this egg has nothing to do with chickens or breakfasts!"

"Obvious to whom?" rumbled Eeyore. "If you don't mind my asking."

"You mean to tell me none of you knows what sort of egg this is?" demanded Rabbit.

"Well," hooted Owl, "it's not an owl egg. I can say that with certainty and not a small amount of relief."

"It's an Easter egg!" Rabbit announced triumphantly.

There was silence as everyone digested this revelation.

"Don't you know?" asked Rabbit. "Easter is a special time, and it's now! This is the time of year everyone gives decorated eggs to one another. I have it on very good authority from my distant cousin, who is a personal acquaintance of someone who knows the Easter Bunny's gardener!"

"Ah!" replied Pooh.

"Why," muttered Eeyore, "would anyone do a thing like give people decorated eggs?"

"Well," Rabbit answered, "it seems, at least from what I've been told, that these are very special eggs."

"Very special how, bunny boy?" Tigger wanted to know.

"It appears," Rabbit said, "that they can talk."

"Ah!" Pooh said again.

"To be specific," Rabbit sniffed importantly, "they are supposed to say how very much we care for one another."

"Hmph," said Gopher, "I bet this egg says it loudly!"

They gathered closely around the egg and listened carefully.

"It's not saying anything," said Tigger.

"P-perhaps it's shy," said Piglet, giving the egg a gentle pat. "I imagine that it feels quite out of place."

"Perhaps if we make it feel at home, it'll feel more like talking," Pooh suggested.

"But how does one make an egg feel at home?" asked Rabbit.

Pooh smiled. "I believe I have an idea."

It seemed as if no time had passed at all before Pooh's plan was put into effect. It appeared as if the giant egg was no longer the only Easter egg Up There.

Pooh was painted pink with blue freckles. Tigger had acquired a checkerboard pattern of pastel colours.

Piglet was very red, while Owl was sky blue. Gopher had become yellow, and Eeyore now had lavender polka dots.

"It has to speak sooner or later, doesn't it?" sighed Pooh. "I mean, if it's going to say it cares about us at all?"

"Maybe we have to tell it how much we care first," suggested Eeyore.

"How do we do that?" asked Piglet.

"The only proper way to speak to an egg," Owl informed everyone, "is when you are sitting on it."

"But," said Tigger, "I wouldn't want anyone sitting on me unless I was pretty sure he knew what he was doing!"

Everyone began rubbing their chins and scratching their heads, furiously trying to work out what they were going to do.

Then Rabbit put his arm around Pooh's shoulders. "This time *I* have a plan, Pooh Bear."

"Ah!" said Pooh.

The next thing Pooh knew, Tigger was standing on top of the egg, tugging on Pooh's paws, while Rabbit stood beneath and pushed for all he was worth. But before anyone could get Pooh seated, let alone ask the egg anything, away it went, rolling down the hill!

They chased the rolling egg downhill and up . . .

through rushing streams and muddy puddles . . .

across wide meadows . . .

under bridges . . .

. . . and over valleys until . . .

the egg slowed down, spun around on its side, and finally stopped . . .

with its tip pointing directly at Christopher Robin!

"What are you doing with my Easter egg?" he asked.

"Delivering it?" Pooh suggested with a smile.

"Well, actually," said Christopher Robin, "this is your egg. All of yours!"

"So when's it going to tell us how much it cares?" Eeyore demanded.

Christopher Robin said, "Watch." He grasped the huge egg and began to twist the top. The egg slowly began to unscrew!

In a moment, Christopher Robin removed the top half of the egg and lifted out another egg painted to look very much like Winnie the Pooh!

One after another, each a bit smaller than the last, an egg in the image of each of Christopher Robin's friends was revealed.

"I'm going to keep mine next to my bedside table," decided Pooh.

"Isn't that a strange place for an Easter egg?" asked Christopher Robin.

"Oh, my goodness, not at all," chuckled Pooh. "Then the last thing it tells me before I fall asleep at night and the first thing it says when I open my eyes in the morning will be how very much somebody cares."

"Happy Easter, silly old bear!"

April Fools' Day

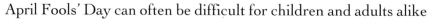

April Fools' Day can often be difficult for children and adults alike because no one seems to know its origin. Also, the idea of being the brunt of a joke is not something anyone looks forward to! The thought of letting down our guard and being made a fool of is fun only when everyone plays. That's what April Fools' Day is really all about.

When Pooh and his friends try to capture the April Fool and play a trick on him, their efforts backfire. They all end up with pies in their faces, flat on their bottoms with buckets of water on their heads. In other words, they learn that on this day, they are all April Fools . . . but, as long as they're laughing together, it's not so bad, after all!

It might be fun to teach a child a simple magic trick for April Fools' Day. By tying the ends of six cotton handkerchiefs together and stuffing them up a sleeve, the child can pretend to blow his or her nose, and then keep pulling the long handkerchief out of the sleeve for a classical comic effect.

Putting on a little magic show is also a nice alternative to practical jokes.

Simple Magic Trick

You will need:
★ Six cotton handkerchiefs (any colour is fine, but coloured ones are fun)

Tie the six handkerchiefs together at the corners, and stuff them from the inside of the shirt or blouse down the sleeve, so just the tip of the first one shows at the cuff. This idea can be greatly exaggerated with more handkerchiefs, tunneling them around the child's back and holding the bulk of them in the opposite sleeve.

Disney's
Winnie the Pooh's
April Fools' Day

Bruce Talkington

Illustrated by Robbin Cuddy

R abbit had called a meeting. Everyone in the Hundred-Acre Wood knew that Rabbit didn't call meetings unless something very significant was afoot. To Rabbit, meetings were as important as honey was to a certain bear with very short legs who was, at that very moment, stumping his way to Rabbit's as quickly as those same very short legs would allow.

Running just as quickly towards the meeting from a quite
different direction (and on legs even shorter than Pooh Bear's)
was Pooh's good friend Piglet.

And Eeyore, carrying his tail in his mouth so as not to lose it
in his hurry, was galloping so rapidly to the gathering (from
yet another direction) that his back legs would occasionally
go faster than his front ones and he would suddenly find himself

running backwards. He would then have to stop and get himself sorted out before his frantic journey could continue.

Gopher was scurrying so rapidly through his tunnels in order to reach the meeting place on time that the trees above ground quaked gently as he jostled their roots in passing.

And high above those trembling treetops, Tigger tore towards the meeting in a series of tremendous bounces.

Meanwhile, Rabbit, at whose house the meeting was to take place, couldn't contain his excitement and was scampering through the woods towards the others to make sure they were all on their way and would not be late.

As a result of this hurrying, scurrying, scampering, galloping, and bouncing, the friends not only were on time for the meeting but were even early! Everyone arrived at a particular crossroads at precisely the same moment, all moving too fast to stop until they'd tumbled head over heels over one another and ended up in a friendly sort of tangle.

"I suppose," sniffed Rabbit after they all had untangled themselves, "that we can call the meeting to order right here and now so Pooh Bear can get on with his assignment."

Pooh's ears perked up in surprise. "As-SIGN-ment?! I'm not very good at making signs, you know. I'm never quite sure why using a certain letter isn't just as good as using one of the others. It's quite confusing."

"This has nothing to do with making signs, Pooh Bear,"
Rabbit said. "It has to do with foolishness, which is why we
need your help."

Rabbit looked down at Pooh and asked, "You do realise
that today is April Fools' Day?"

"Of course," laughed Pooh, delighted to know the right
answer for a change. "It's the one day of the year you can
look like a fool and not feel unhappy about it."

"Well, I suggest that this year we not be fooled," sniffed Rabbit, looking very determined.

"Might be nice for a change," said Tigger, with a grin. "We certainly do a stupenderous job of looking pretty silly the entire rest of the year."

"But today it's someone else's turn!" cackled Gopher.

"Really?" asked Pooh. "Whose turn is it?"

"I think Rabbit means he wants us to fool the April Fool before he fools us!" Piglet whispered into Pooh's ear.

Pooh leaned close to his friends and whispered, "How are we going to do it?"

Rabbit whispered back, "You're going to find the April Fool and bring him to my house."

"I am?" asked Pooh in amazement.

"But be careful, Pooh," warned Piglet. "I've heard that the April Fool can look like anybody!"

"He can?" gasped Pooh.

"Absolutely," whistled Gopher. "That's how he fools you!"

"Don't worry, Pooh," Tigger assured Pooh with a slap on the back. "You'll find him. Nobody knows more about foolishness than you do."

As the others hurried off to Rabbit's house to prepare their surprise for the April Fool, Pooh scratched his head furiously with both hands. It didn't help. He hadn't the faintest idea of where to start looking for the April Fool — or what to do with him if he found him.

All at once Pooh recalled that fool rhymed with pool. He proceeded immediately to the largest collection of water in the forest — a quiet pond near the river. As Pooh cautiously crossed from one side of this pool to the other on a series of stepping-stones, the one that happened to be a turtle and not a rock tipped him headfirst into the water.

Sitting on the bottom of the pool, Pooh was, needless to say, thoroughly disappointed. There was not a single fool to be found.

So Pooh began to look in places that didn't rhyme with fool.

All he found in a cave were some pesky echoes that loved to make fools of people but were not precisely foolish themselves. They were not precisely anything, really, except a lot of noise, and Pooh, who was very well acquainted with the likes of Rabbit and Eeyore and

Owl, knew that a lot of noise didn't make one foolish . . .
most of the time. And the bats that all this noise
awakened hadn't any interest in fools, only in chasing
Pooh away so they could go back to sleep. Pooh
managed to escape by plunging back into the pool and
sitting on the bottom until the grumpy bats flew back to
their cave.

And when Pooh poked his nose into a certain large hollow tree, he was suddenly swamped by an avalanche of acorns left over from a squirrel's winter storage. Slipping and sliding, Pooh found himself sitting down hard in the pool once again.

Exhausted and quite damp, Pooh scrunched his face up into a painful frown. He was positive his friends were right in thinking that he could find the April Fool because foolishness was, after all, something with which he had a great deal of experience. Besides that, he couldn't remember his friends ever being wrong.

Pooh sighed and unscrewed his face. "Perhaps I should go to
Rabbit's house and ask for help," he said to himself. But he
immediately shook his head. "No, that would be foolish. They're
busy getting ready to fool the April Fool."

All at once Pooh sat up straight, and a smile lit up his face.

"If it's foolish to go to Rabbit's," Pooh exclaimed, "then that's
where the April Fool will be!"

Without wasting another moment, Pooh set off as fast as his
dripping legs could carry him.

At Rabbit's house, everyone was ready for the arrival of the April Fool.

Rabbit had set a huge bucket of water over his front door to spill onto the Fool's head when he entered.

Piglet was nearby with a very small, yet very tasty, cream pie he'd made from his favourite recipe to toss into the Fool's face.

Off to one side stood Tigger with a huge pepper shaker to sprinkle on the Fool's nose and make him sneeze.

The small rug by the front door was clamped firmly in Eeyore's mouth to be yanked out from under the Fool's feet.

Finally, Gopher was prepared to spill a bag of fluffy feathers that would cling to the damp Fool and cause him to resemble a giant chicken!

The gang was ready for everything except for what happened next.

The front door flew open, and there stood Winnie
the Pooh, shouting "April Fool!" at the top of his voice.

The horrified Rabbit tried to save Pooh from the
falling bucket of water but succeeded only in getting
it jammed over his own head, which caused him to
stumble about blindly.

He bumped into Tigger, who staggered backwards

and sat in Piglet's pie, accidentally sprinkling his pepper into Eeyore's nose.

Eeyore, still hanging on to the rug, emitted such a powerful sneeze that it propelled him backwards into Gopher, who spilled his feathers all over Piglet as the rug jerked out from under Pooh's feet and set the bear down on the ground with a loud thump.

After a moment of shocked silence Pooh finally managed to blurt out, "The April Fool is here!" Then he looked down at his still-dripping jersey. "But he did seem to be very much out there, too."

Then the laughter began. And it was quite a while before anyone could speak.

Finally, Rabbit, wiping the tears of mirth from his eyes, put his arm around Pooh's shoulders and said, "I think you've discovered the Fool's secret, Pooh Bear!"

"I have?"

"It seems the April Fool," hooted Tigger, "looks just like us!"

"And a good thing, too," sighed Pooh.

"Why's that, Pooh Bear?" demanded Piglet, trying to remove a particularly large feather from his very small ear.

"Because then we can all laugh with one another — and not at anyone," said Pooh. "Or am I being foolish?"

"No, Pooh," said Piglet with a smile. "Not this time."

And the laughter began again and went on and on for a very long time.

Halloween

Halloween has always been something of a monument to make-believe. Children love dressing up in masks and costumes on the last day in October. It's also a wonderful time for parents to help children explore fears that may be somewhat out of context during the rest of the year. Dark rooms are a perennial issue; so are shadows, stairs, and strange noises. However, at Halloween, those shadows on the wall can be made into a game. Who can make the scariest shapes?

A project where children make simple masks can actually help *unmask* certain fears. When children draw the scary faces on them themselves, they can decide whether they want it to look scary or not. In this story, Pooh and friends find a way to celebrate Halloween together and Piglet discovers that confronting his Halloween fears head-on, with help from his friends, is sometimes the best way to deal with them.

Mask-making

You will need:

* large paper plates (the ones with fluted or scalloped edges are fine)
* water-based marker pens
* cotton wool balls
* glue
* wooden lollipop sticks (most craft shops should sell them)
* scissors
* glitter

Cut eyes, nose, and mouth openings from paper plates. Glue wooden lollipop sticks to the bottom of the mask so they can be handheld. Decorate with markers, cotton, and glitter and let the children's imaginations run wild!

Disney's

Winnie the Pooh's Halloween

Bruce Talkington

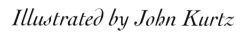

Illustrated by John Kurtz

The late afternoon sun appeared to hesitate on the horizon, settling comfortably among the tip-top branches of the trees in the Hundred-Acre Wood.

"Look," chuckled Winnie the Pooh from the grassy clearing where he and his friends were watching the sunset. "The sun doesn't want to go to bed!"

"Perhaps it's afraid of the dark," suggested Piglet, who was much fonder of the sun's arriving than he was of its going to bed.

Christopher Robin put his arm comfortingly around Piglet's shoulders. "No, Piglet," he explained, "the sun simply wants to stay and share Halloween with us."

"Oh?" remarked Pooh Bear, his tummy grumbling. "Is Halloween, perhaps, a very small smackeral of something sweet" — he licked his lips hopefully — "to eat?"

"Don't be silly, Pooh Bear," snorted Rabbit. "A Halloween isn't something to eat."

"Of course not," agreed Tigger, bouncing up and down on his coiled tail. "Everybody knows that."

"Pardon me for saying so," interrupted Eeyore, "but knowing what something *isn't* doesn't exactly tell us what something *is*, which seems to me to be the point, if that's what we're looking for. The point, I mean."

"Never mind the point," whistled Gopher. "All I want to know is what on earth we're talking about!"

"Halloween," announced Pooh, proud of himself for remembering.

"And what exactly is a Halloween?" demanded Gopher.

The friends exchanged shrugs and puzzled frowns, then turned to Christopher Robin for an answer.

"Halloween," Christopher Robin informed them excitedly, "is the scariest time of year — because it takes place at night."

"If you don't mind," responded Piglet, trying to keep his ears from trembling, "I think I'll be thinking as little as possible about scary things that happen in the dark."

"But that's what Halloween is," protested Christopher Robin. "When the sun goes down, we all dress up and see who can be the scariest."

Piglet noticed the sun was no longer resting comfortably in the treetops but was, in fact, almost out of sight behind the horizon.

"Uh, I'm sorry, but I won't have time to play Halloween with you," Piglet blurted out. "I have some very important things to do."

"What could be more important than scaring each other in the dark?" Tigger asked.

"Turning on every light in my house and dusting under my bed," said Piglet, hurrying away into the dusk.

"Poor Piglet," sighed Christopher Robin. "We've frightened him. But I suppose he can suit himself."

"And that's just what I'm going to do," laughed Tigger, bouncing around his friends in excited circles. "Suit myself up in the most fantastical costume I can think of!"

As the all others shouted their agreement, Pooh was strangely silent.

"What's the matter, Pooh Bear?" Christopher Robin asked as they all scattered to prepare their costumes.

"Well," Pooh said sadly, "I suppose I'm going to miss sharing Halloween with my best friend, Piglet."

"Never mind," comforted Christopher Robin. "You're simply going to have to have twice as much fun as everyone else and share it with him later."

"What a good idea!" exclaimed Pooh. "And I'll have to be twice as scary, too."

"You'd better get started on your costume then," laughed Christopher Robin.

"Oh, yes," Pooh mused. "My costume."

Pooh remembered that his scariest experiences were whenever he visited the honey tree for an extra smackeral before, or after, whatever meal it happened to be. (Eating always made Pooh very hungry.)

"Nothing is scarier than a honeybee," Pooh decided, "so that's what I'm going to be . . . a BEE!"

When Pooh arrived home, he immediately opened up his chest of odds and ends of no possible use to anyone except to a bear of very little brain, and began to look for his costume.

In no time at all Pooh
was ready.

With black paint,
he had painted thick
stripes around his
middle.

He stuck a plunger to
his bottom with a small sign
attached saying "Stinger"
so everyone would
know he was a bee.

On his head went Pooh's answer to antennae — two wobbly springs topped with ping-pong balls.

"That," Pooh said to himself as he examined his image in the mirror, "is very frightening indeed!"

Pooh hurried out to meet his friends. No one would be better suited for Halloween than he.

The night had become quite dark. Pooh would have walked right over Gopher without seeing him, but then he noticed two glowing eyes peering out of the gloom.

"Well?" Gopher's voice demanded. "What do you think?"

Pooh had to look very closely to distinguish his practically invisible friend. He was wrapped head to foot in a billowing black cloak.

"Gopher!" Pooh exclaimed. "You certainly surprised me!"

"I knew I would!" Gopher laughed. "Nothing's spookier than a dark night, so that's what I decided to be. Scared myself out of a week's sleep when I looked in the mirror. I love Halloween!"

Before Pooh and Gopher could discuss their costumes further, Tigger dropped very suddenly out of the night sky and landed between them. Then, with a loud "Hoo-hoo-HOO!" he squirted them both with a water pistol.

"Tigger!" spluttered Pooh, rubbing the water out of his eyes and gazing at his friend in wonder.

Tigger had donned a bright-red jersey emblazoned with a wriggly bolt of yellow lightning.

"Who are you?" asked Gopher.

"You know the rainstorm everyone's so afraid is going to come?" Tigger asked. "Well, I'm here! Scary, aren't I?"

"Not to me," rumbled a voice from behind them.

All three spun around in surprise. "Eeyore!" they shouted.

Eeyore was wearing a large red nose as well as a yellow ruffled collar around his neck. On his head was perched the pointiest clown's hat anyone had ever seen topped by a feathery orange ball.

"I was afraid if I were too frightening, I'd have to spend Halloween alone," Eeyore explained. "I Hope I didn't frighten anyone too badly."

Pooh reassured him. "If I hadn't heard your friendly voice first, I'm sure I would be running for my life this very moment."

"I don't really believe you," said Eeyore sadly. Then a smile spread over his face. "But I'm going to because it makes me feel better!"

The four friends began a long,

loud laugh that stopped very suddenly when they saw Rabbit staring at them in annoyance.

"What are you laughing at?" Rabbit wanted to know. "This is the most frightening costume I could think of."

Rabbit had stuck clumps of cotton wool all over himself.

"Perhaps it would be more frightening," suggested Eeyore gently, "if you told us what you are."

Rabbit leaned close and whispered, "A big ball of dust!" and shuddered at the thought. "There's nothing more frightening to me than those little balls of dust with minds of their own collecting where I can't get a broom to them!"

The thought of wayward dust suddenly reminded Pooh of Piglet huddled alone under his bed.

"I'm sure Piglet would be terrified of your costume, Rabbit," said Pooh sadly.

Before Rabbit could respond, however, a long, low moan sounded, rattling ominously out of the darkness, causing everyone to stiffen in surprise.

"Wooooooooooooooooooo!"

"What was that?" Tigger whispered.

"I don't think I want to wait to see this costume," said Rabbit with a shiver.

"Wooooooooooooooooooo!"

Another moan drifted out of the blackness under the trees.

"I think we should go to Piglet's," suggested Pooh, "and make sure he's not too frightened."

"You're right, Pooh. That's what friends are for. Last one to Piglet's house is . . . not first!" shouted Tigger.

The friends ran headlong through the Hundred-Acre Wood. In the distance Piglet's house had every light ablaze and shone like a beacon to guide weary travellers home.

Tigger threw open Piglet's front door and ran inside, followed closely by Rabbit, Gopher, and Pooh, with a panting Eeyore bringing up the rear.

Thundering across Piglet's gleaming floor, they all tried to stop, but the hours of careful waxing proved their downfall. Skidding through the house, they all slipped onto their sides and slid in a tangle to end up in a pile under Piglet's bed!

"Piglet?" Pooh called out.

"Wooooooooooooooooooo!" sounded the answer.

"The scary thing's got Piglet!" Pooh whispered.

"No it hasn't," answered Piglet. Then the bedspread lifted, and Piglet joined them under the bed. "The scary thing didn't get me. The scary thing IS me!"

"Who would have guessed," Pooh laughed, "that the scariest costume turned out to be no costume at all?"

"You see," Piglet explained, "I was so scared about being scared that I knew the only way Halloween was going to be bearable for me was if I was the most frightening one of all!"

"And you did a stupendous job," laughed Tigger, patting Piglet on the back. "But what do we do now?"

"Well," said Pooh thoughtfully. "Why don't we stay with piglet and have Halloween here?"

"And hot chocolate," suggested Eeyore.

"And tell scary stories," added Tigger.

"Excellent!" announced Rabbit. "I'll go first. Once upon a time, there was a giant ball of dust . . ."

As Rabbit continued, Pooh put his arm around Piglet's shoulders.

"I think I like Halloween, Pooh Bear," Piglet whispered to his friend.

"Me, too, Piglet," Pooh whispered back as he huddled closer. "Me, too!"

Thanksgiving

Thanksgiving is a festival celebrated, mostly in America, in November. It is a time to give thanks for all the good things around us. In reading the adventures of Winnie the Pooh we are charmed by Pooh's generous nature. This, of course, seems in direct conflict to his passion for possessing "hunny." Pooh is a bear who will always offer whatever is in his cupboard to anyone who comes to his door. Pooh's generosity, in the light of his insatiable appetite, is what makes him so endearing. He possesses an unconditional love for his friends.

In this story, Pooh and friends enjoy Thanksgiving together, and Christopher Robin shares what he is most thankful for: having Pooh Bear and all his friends to share his day with.

The focus of Thanksgiving is a traditional meal, a bit like Christmas dinner. Children could create place cards for guests, and decorate them to reflect the things that they are most thankful for.

Walnut Place Cards

You will need:
- ★ coloured card
- ★ water-based marker pens
- ★ glue
- ★ glitter
- ★ scissors
- ★ whole walnuts (in the shell)

Cut shapes from the coloured card. You could draw them freehand or trace them from a book or magazine — try hearts, stars or flowers. Write the names of the guests on the cards, leaving room to decorate the border using glitter and marker pens. When the cards are ready, carefully take one of the scissor blades, gently pry a little space in the seam of the walnut, and insert the name cards. Ask an adult to help you do this.

DISNEY'S

Winnie the Pooh's Thanksgiving

Bruce Talkington

Illustrated by John Kurtz

W here can he be?"
Rabbit said in his
most frustrated
I-really-want-to-know voice.
It was the question that
was in the mind of everyone
standing at Winnie the Pooh's
front door. The thoroughly
annoyed Rabbit once again
rapped loudly on the door,
which continued to stand
unopened no matter how
vigorously he knocked.

Tigger was sitting back on his tail with his face flattened against the glass of Pooh's window.

"There's nothing moving in there," he informed the others.

"That doesn't mean a great deal," rumbled Eeyore from where he was seated on a nearby patch of grass. "Not moving is one of the things Pooh Bear does best. Next to snoring."

"And eating honey," added little Roo excitedly. "Isn't that right, Mum?"

"Yes, dear," Kanga said as she smiled down at him and gently straightened his fur with her hand.

"Why would Pooh ask us here if he were somewhere else?" whistled Gopher, scratching his head.

Piglet stood wringing his very small hands worriedly. "Oh, dear," he sighed, "I do hope he's alright."

"Now let's not jump to conclusions," Kanga spoke up gently. "If I remember correctly," Kanga continued, "Pooh Bear simply asked us to meet him. He didn't mention where."

"Very nice of him, too," remarked Eeyore. "He obviously didn't want us to feel bad if we couldn't find the right place, so he kept the location a secret."

"Now," Rabbit sighed, "if we could only think of the place where Pooh is!"

"Perhaps you just did," said Eeyore. "Pooh was certainly thinking about something when he called us together."

". . . an' Pooh always does his best head work . . ." continued Tigger.

". . . in his very own Thoughtful Spot!" finished Piglet.

And that is exactly where they found Winnie the Pooh, high up on the grassy hill, with its spectacular view of the Hundred-Acre Wood, where Pooh loved to sit and think. It was the sitting in such a special place that was important, after all, not the thinking.

And there was no doubt as to what Pooh was being thoughtful about. It was all spread out on a blanket before him. Pooh's kitchen must have been completely emptied because he had carried everything sweet and tasty from his house to the grassy hill and arranged it all to look most delicious.

"I'm so very glad you've come," sighed Winnie the Pooh happily. "I don't think this food could have waited much longer."

"And neither could I," he added with a smile.

"Then let's not waste a moment more," said Rabbit, and they all sat down to eat.

"I'm very glad to see you at last," said Pooh. "I hope I haven't brought too much to eat."

"No such thing as too many eats when eatin' is the name o' the game," chuckled Tigger as he hungrily rubbed his paws together.

"Is eating the only reason you called us together, Pooh Bear?" asked Owl.

"Called you together where?" responded Pooh, tucking his tongue carefully into the corner of his mouth as he pulled the stopper on a fresh pot of honey because, as everyone knows, a stopper cannot be properly pulled if a tongue is not tactfully tucked.

"Why, called us here, Pooh," squeaked Roo.

"Did I do that?" said Pooh, so surprised by the idea that he waited an extra second or two before pouring an extra-large dollop of honey into his mouth.

"You certainly did," answered Gopher. "And what we want to know is why you did it!"

"Not that it wasn't an excellent idea, Pooh dear," Kanga added gently.

"Well," murmured Pooh in a thoughtful sort of voice as he gently tugged on an ear with his honey-smeared paw, "it must have begun this morning when I sat down for breakfast."

Pooh explained how he was
suddenly very much aware of
how special a breakfast could
be because, like so very many
things — sunsets and birthdays,

surprises and snooze times,
hugs and extra pudding —
a breakfast was more than
just today. It was an
always-there-when-a-bear-
needed-it sort of thing.

"You mean you were grateful, Pooh?" asked Piglet in a very quiet voice when his friend had finished.

"Why, yes, Piglet," smiled Pooh. "That's it exactly. And it was such a wonderful thank-you-very-much feeling, and so very, very

large, that I knew it was something I had to share with those
I'm most grateful for."

"And what sort of 'those' do you mean, Pooh?" wondered Owl.

"Why, you all, of course," exclaimed Pooh. "My very best and dearest friends!"

"Well," sniffed Rabbit, "I'm certainly grateful that you thought of it."

"And what are you grateful for, Piglet?" Pooh inquired politely as he put his arm around his friend's very small shoulders.

"Well," began Piglet nervously, and then continued in a rush, "for a very small animal, I have a great deal to be grateful for. And having a lot to be grateful for is, when you come right

down to it, a lot to be grateful for!" Piglet finished, quite out
of breath.

Rabbit explained that what he was mostly thankful for
(besides his many very good friends, of course) was that a seed
had the extremely good sense to sprout when he planted it in
his garden.

"And *I'm* grateful that the ground looks as good from under-
neath as it does from on top," whistled Gopher. "Yes sirree!"

Tigger expressed his gratitude that down-ing through the air was just as splendiferous as up-ping.

"The item for which I am, indeed, most thankful," announced Owl in his most dignified voice, "is that I always remember in the nick of time to land on my feet and not on my face."

"I'm grateful just for the chance to be grateful," rumbled Eeyore. "If that's alright with everyone, that is."

Everyone agreed that it was, indeed, quite alright with them.

Kanga and little Roo said they were grateful for each other at exactly the same time.

And at that very moment Christopher Robin arrived quite out of breath and said, "I'm terribly sorry to be so late, Pooh Bear. What exactly are we all doing up here?"

"We're having a feast and telling each other what we are grateful for," said Pooh.

Then Pooh surveyed the blanket and realised that there wasn't a single smackeral of anything left to eat.

"You missed the feast part, I'm afraid," he told Christopher Robin sadly.

"That's alright," laughed Christopher Robin. "I can still do the other."

Then he stood up straight and began to speak in a very grown-up voice.

"I'm very grateful for having the opportunity of finding you all here together so I can invite you to join me for Thanksgiving dinner."

"Thanksgiving dinner!" exclaimed everyone all at once. "What's that?"

"Well, you all already know the most important part," laughed Christopher Robin. "It's a special time when all the things we're grateful for throughout the year have their very own day to celebrate with us!"

"What a nice idea," said Pooh with a satisfied smile. "I'd like to thank whoever thought of it."

"You thought of it all by yourself, you silly bear!" laughed Tigger as he slapped Pooh on the back.

"Ah," said Pooh with a grin, "the dinner part did sound familiar. And you did mention . . . dinner?" Pooh checked carefully.

"All you can eat . . . and more," Christopher Robin assured him.

"Isn't it wonderful," said Pooh as he rubbed his tummy, "that Thanksgiving dinner is something we're all warmed up for?"

Everyone agreed that it was, indeed, quite wonderful.

"Another thing," said Pooh quietly, "to be so very grateful for."

Christmas

Pooh, being a bear of little brain, typically gets to the heart of things in a roundabout way. In this delightful tale, he finds himself on Christmas Eve without any presents for his friends. People often forget what Christmas is about and find themselves apologising for a small gift by saying, "Well, it's the thought that counts." In truth, the thought *is* really all that matters. In this story, Pooh discovers that the value of a Christmas present, like beauty, is in the eye of the beholder. Intending to return before dawn, Pooh Bear tiptoes through the night placing Christmas stockings in the homes of his sleeping friends. When he accidentally falls asleep before filling the stockings with presents, the outcome is pure Christmas magic.

Underscoring the message that this season is all about giving, a fun activity might be sewing simple Christmas stockings. You could either decorate old socks that you no longer use, or make new ones from felt, or any fabric.

Christmas Stockings

You will need:

* several pieces of coloured felt (you can buy this from craft shops)
* glue
* glitter
* hole punch
* red and green thread
* large, blunt craft needle
* scissors

Cut stocking shapes from the felt and sew together with contrasting coloured thread. For younger children, punch sewing holes along the edges of the stockings to guide them. Decorate with glitter by drizzling glue in patterns and sprinkling glitter on top. Allow at least an hour to dry thoroughly.

DISNEY'S

Winnie the Pooh's
Christmas

Bruce Talkington

Illustrated by Alvin S. White Studio

It was the night before Christmas, and Winnie the Pooh's nose was pressed flat against the window. He was gazing out at the snowflakes falling in the Hundred-Acre Wood, gathering like bedclothes around his house.

"I'm very glad to see you," Pooh whispered to the plump snowflakes drifting past. "You're just in time for Christmas, which, if you must be in time for something, is something very special to be in time for!"

Pooh turned to take a look at his house, full of decorations. "Let me see, a tree, some candles . . ." He scratched his head and sighed. "There seems to be something . . . missing!"

All at once Pooh heard a series of very small knocks at his front door. "Perhaps," Pooh smiled to himself, "that is whatever it is that's missing!"

Pooh opened the door to find a very small snowman with a pair of very Piglet-looking ears.

"Oh!" remarked Pooh, who was a very surprised bear. Then
he added "Hello!" to be polite, because one should always be
polite, even to surprises.

"H-h-hello, P-Pooh B-Bear," the snowman answered in a
very Piglet-sounding voice. "M-Merry Christmas!"

Pooh wondered whether it was more polite to invite the snowman in where it was warm or let him stay outside where snowmen are usually more comfortable. The snowman finally gave Pooh a very small hint. "May I come in?" it asked.

"Please do," said Pooh.

The snowman hurried inside and stood in front of the fire. "The only thing I don't like about Christmas," said the snowman, "and it's a very small thing, is that my ears get so very cold."

"I can imagine," replied Pooh, who could not imagine a snowman's ears being anything but cold.

The snowman stood shivering in front of the fire and, with every tremble and quiver, began to look less and less like a snowman and more and more like Piglet.

"Why, hello, Piglet!" blurted Pooh, delighted to see his very best friend standing in a puddle of water. "If I had known it was you, I would have invited you in!"

Piglet smiled up at his friend. "Oh, Pooh! You did invite me in! You knew it was me all along."

"Well, of course I did, Piglet," responded Pooh.

"My!" breathed Piglet in wonder as he gazed up at Pooh's Christmas tree. "I've never seen so many candles on one tree."

"Well," explained Pooh, "there seemed to be a great
many empty honey pots to use for candle-holders. And
there was a great deal of extra room on the tree because
the popcorn didn't seem to get strung."

"Would you like me to help you string the popcorn,
Pooh?" Piglet asked.

"Why, yes, Piglet. I'd like that very much," answered
Pooh. "That is, if there were any popcorn left to string,

which there isn't."

"Oh, dear," said Piglet. He looked around nervously,
leaned close to Pooh, and whispered, "What happened to
it all?"

"I ate it," Pooh whispered back. "I was tasting it to
make sure it was properly popped, and by the time I was
sure," Pooh shrugged and sighed, "it was all gone. I do,
however, still have the string."

"That's alright, Pooh!" Piglet laughed. "We can use the string to wrap your presents!"

"But, Piglet," explained Pooh, "the presents won't be here until tomorrow morning. And then I *unwrap* them." Pooh leaned close and whispered confidentially into Piglet's ear. "That's the way it's done, you know." There may have been a few things about Christmas on which Pooh was a little hazy, but opening presents wasn't one of them.

"No, Pooh, I mean I'll help you wrap the presents you're going to *give*!"

Pooh's smile disappeared. "Oh!" he said quietly. "*Those* gifts." Then even more quietly, he added, "Oh, bother!"

"What's the matter, Pooh?" Piglet asked.

Pooh sighed. "I think I've just remembered what I forgot," he said. "It's presents."

"No presents?" Piglet looked up at Pooh sadly.

"Not even a very small one?"

Pooh shook his head. "I'm sorry, Piglet."

Piglet smiled bravely. "It's alright, Pooh. I always get a bit too excited opening presents. And it's the thought that counts, you know," he sniffed. "I think I'll take my very cold ears and go home."

Pooh saw his friend to the door and watched him walk sadly down the path as the snowflakes began turning him into a very small snowman once again.

"Oh dear," Pooh said to himself as he wound his scarf around his neck and stepped out into the snow. "If it's the thought that counts at Christmas, I think I'd better ask Christopher Robin what he thinks about thoughts and presents and Christmas and everything."

It was a long, chilly walk through the swirling snowy night.
The snowflakes tickled Pooh's nose and crept down the back of
his neck. He was very glad when he arrived at Christopher
Robin's house, and he knocked loudly on the door.

"Pooh Bear!" Christopher Robin exclaimed. "What a lovely surprise! Come in!"

Christopher Robin led Pooh into the toasty-warm house, ablaze with lights and colours dancing merrily from candles to glass balls to tinsel and back again!

"My!" Pooh breathed. "This certainly looks Christmassy! So I suppose I can ask you what I came to find out" — he rubbed his chin thoughtfully — "as soon as I remember what it is."

But then Pooh stepped up to Christopher Robin's fireplace, where a row of stockings in all shapes and sizes hung neatly from the mantelpiece.

"Don't you think," Pooh remarked, "that Christmas is, perhaps, not the best time for drying socks?"

"Silly old bear," Christopher Robin laughed, ruffling the fluff on Pooh's head. "That's not my laundry. They're stockings to hold Christmas presents!"

"You mean," Pooh answered slowly, "you have to have stockings to put presents in?"

"Yes," said Christopher Robin, "that's the way it's done."

"Oh, bother!" said Pooh, looking down at his feet. Not only

did he have no presents for his friends, but he had no stockings to put the no presents in! Pooh, being a bear, had little use for stockings. Pooh told Christopher Robin that he thought all his friends in the Hundred-Acre Wood were much the same way.

Christopher Robin laughed. "Come with me, Pooh Bear. I have plenty of stockings for everyone."

Christopher Robin showed Pooh a drawer containing socks and stockings of every size, shape, and colour.

"These are all stockings that have lost their mates and would love to have someone to share Christmas with," said Christopher Robin. He scratched one of Pooh's ears. "It's the thought that counts, you know."

"Why, yes," replied Pooh, happy that Christopher Robin had remembered to answer the question that he had forgotten to ask. "Thank you very much, Christopher Robin."

Soon Pooh was walking happily home with his arms full of stockings. The snow had stopped falling, leaving a wonderful white blanket over the entire forest. It was as if the Hundred-Acre Wood had decorated itself for Christmas. A huge moon made it seem as bright as day.

"But," Pooh reminded himself with a yawn, "it is very late, and I must get these stockings delivered." He thought for a moment. "I must get everyone presents, too, of course, but the stockings come first."

And so Pooh, being as quiet as the soft night around him, crept into his friends' homes one by one, and left a stocking hanging from each one's mantelpiece with a little note attached saying, "From Pooh".

First, of course, there was Piglet's house, where Pooh placed
a very small stocking.

He then left a striped one for Tigger because he was sure that
was the sort of stocking Tiggers like best.

Pooh left a very bright
orange one at Rabbit's
house.

Eeyore got the
warmest and
friendliest stocking
Pooh could find.

Gopher received a long, dark stocking. Pooh thought it was
what a tunnel would look like if a tunnel were a stocking.

Finally, Owl was given a stocking the colour of the sky — in which, Pooh thought, he would like to fly if he were Owl.

It was very, very late when Pooh nailed his own
honey-coloured stocking to his very own mantelpiece.

"Now that this stocking business is all taken care of," said
Pooh, settling down in his softest armchair, "I simply must do
some serious thinking about what I am going to give my friends
for Christmas." Pooh closed his eyes, and soon neither his
snoring nor the sun rising over the Hundred-Acre Wood
disturbed his thoughts.

In fact, Pooh did not stop his deep thinking — or loud snoring — until a knock sounded at his door, accompanied by a chorus of "Merry Christmas, Pooh Bear!"

Pooh opened his eyes and glanced about anxiously.

"Oh, no," he thought. "My friends are here for
Christmas and I have no presents for any of them!"

"There's only one thing to do," he told himself. "I shall
simply have to tell my friends I'm sorry, but I only *thought*
about presents for them, and didn't actually *get* them."

Pooh opened his door and started to apologise, but before he could say a word, in rushed all his friends — Piglet, Tigger, Rabbit, Gopher, Eeyore, and Owl — all thanking Pooh at once for his thoughtful gifts.

Piglet was wearing a new stocking cap. "My ears are very grateful, Pooh Bear. It was exactly what I wanted."

Tigger told Pooh how much he loved his new stripedy
sleeping bag. "It's cosier than cosy!"

Rabbit couldn't wait to explain how he'd always dreamed
of owning a colour-coordinated carrot cover. How could
Pooh possibly have known?

Gopher appreciated the "bag" for toting around his rock
samples. "Never had one big enough before," he said.

Eeyore explained — if anyone was interested — that his tail
had never been warmer than it was in its new warmer.

Owl was positive his brand-new "wind sock" would provide him with all the necessary data required to prevent the occasional crash landing through his dining room window!

188

Pooh put his hands behind his back and looked thoughtful.
"Something awfully nice is going on, though I'm not at all sure
how it happened."

"I'll tell you how it happened, buddy bear," exclaimed Tigger.
"It's called Christmas!" He shoved a large pot of honey, with a
stripedy ribbon and bow, into the stocking hanging from Pooh's
mantelpiece. The others quickly followed suit with presents of
their own for Pooh, which all turned out to be pots of honey.
What else would a Pooh Bear want for Christmas . . . or any
other time?

"Christmas," sighed Pooh happily. "What a very sweet thought, indeed!"